SCAREDY BOOK

It's not always easy to be brave!

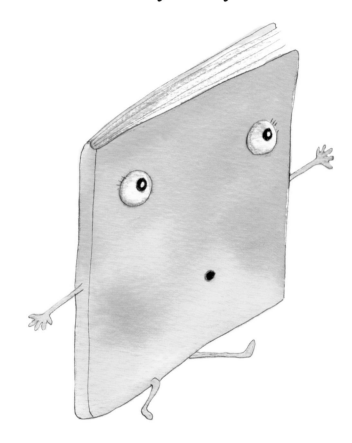

DEVON SILLETT & CARA KING

For Aaron and Jay — May you never cease to
venture to the library and beyond. For Auntie
Carol and Adina — May your shelves grow
ever larger, and your skies ever taller.
— D.S.

For my adventure-loving family, Pete,
Charlie and Angus. You are precious.
— C.K.

First published 2018

EK Books
an imprint of Exisle Publishing Pty Ltd
PO Box 864, Chatswood, NSW 2057, Australia
226 High Street, Dunedin, 9016, New Zealand
www.ekbooks.org

A CiP record for this book is available from the National
Library of Australia.

ISBN 978-1-925335-68-2

Designed by Big Cat Design
Typeset in Minya Nouvelle 21 on 28pt
Printed in China

This book uses paper sourced under ISO 14001 guidelines
from well-managed forests and other controlled sources.

10 9 8 7 6 5 4 3 2 1

Book was full of potential.

But sometimes, a pinch of pizazz, a sprinkling of gumption and a drop of courage come in handy.

Book wished to have all those things. But Library was very, very comfortable.

And warm.

And peaceful.

Safe.

In short, Book loved his nook.

From where he perched, Book could watch the others skip out the door.

They experienced great adventures.

Made new friends.

And returned to tell the tale.

Book thought he might like to try new things, too. He came close a few times.

Well, maybe close was stretching it.
But Book thought about coming close.

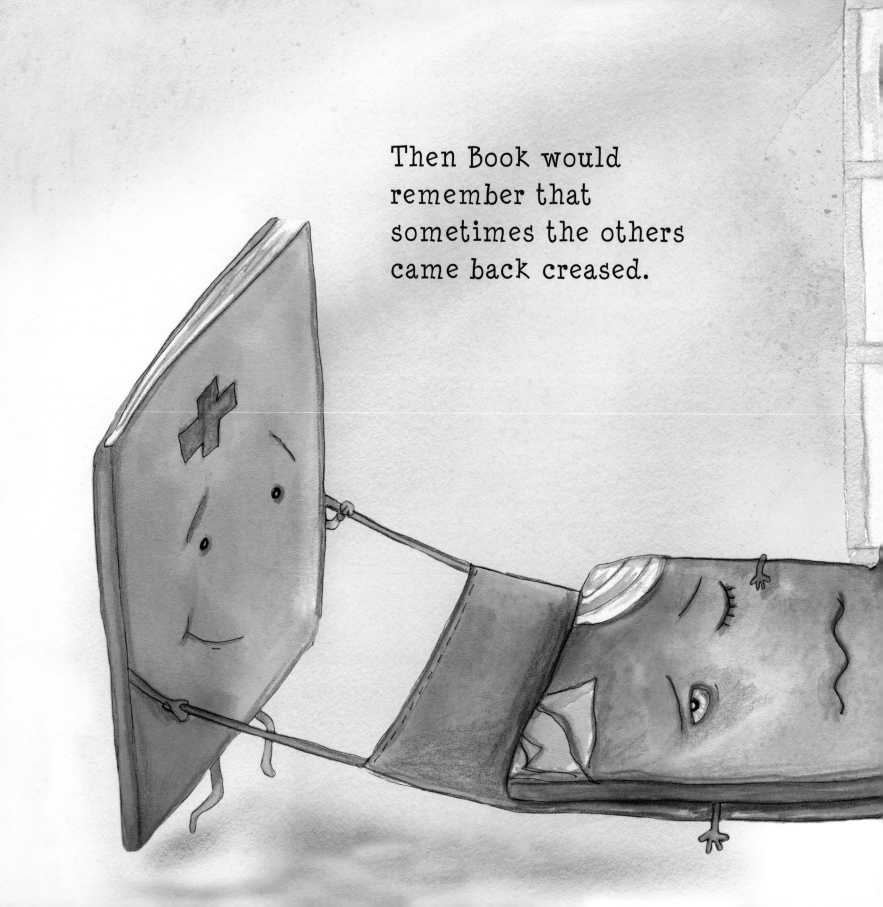

Then Book would remember that sometimes the others came back creased.

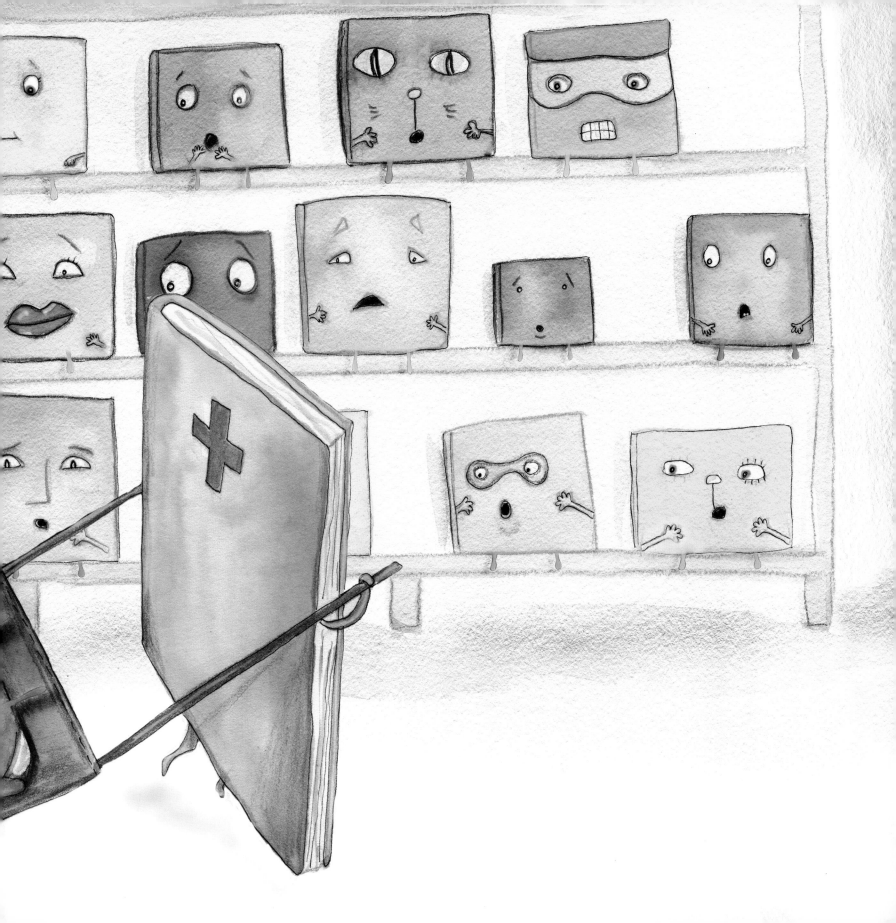

Or sticky.

Or ripped.

Once, one returned with two missing pages.

The pages were never found.

MISSING
HAVE YOU SEEN

C

THIS BOOK?

Occasionally, one of the others never returned at all.

Book wanted to go out very badly.
To feel sunlight on his pages.

Dance in a puddle or two.

Maybe even kick a ball.

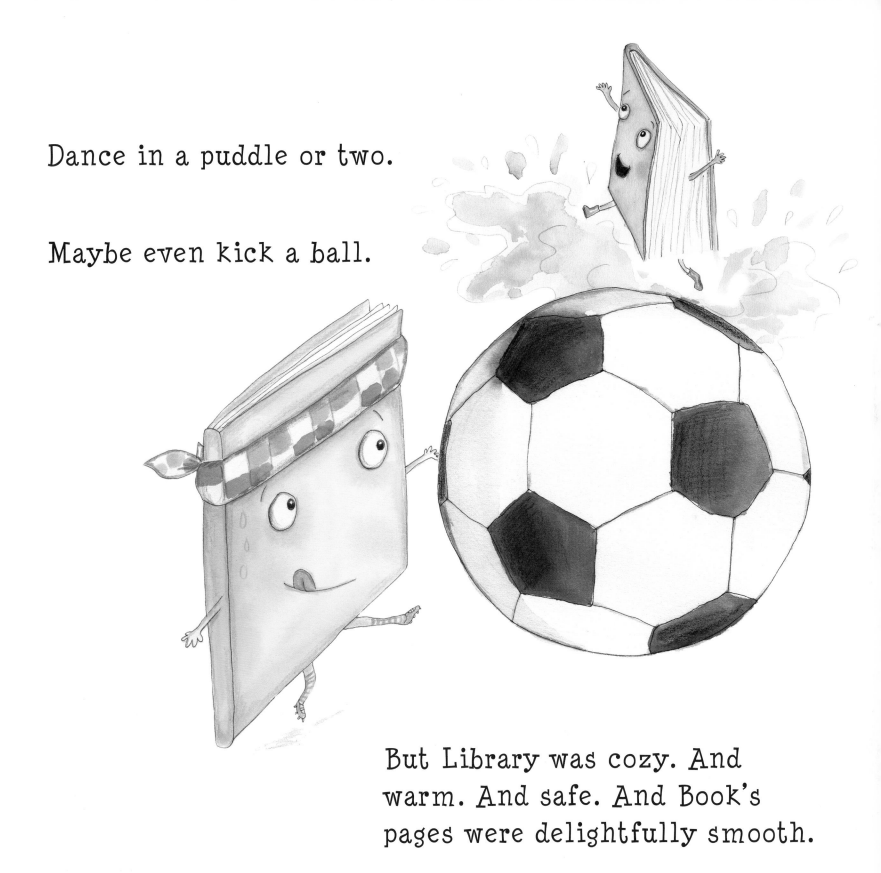

But Library was cozy. And
warm. And safe. And Book's
pages were delightfully smooth.

Library was Emma's favourite place, too.

Emma went on many great adventures.

Clashed with giants. Fought off dragons and snakes. Rescued fair maidens and hapless princes. Or relaxed atop a tower of beds with a teeny, tiny pea underneath.

Emma was quiet, but full of pizazz.
Gumption.
Courage.

But Emma and Book seemed destined
never to meet. Until one day, Book found
a little drop of courage in his spine.

Emma was worried about Book.

He looked a little faded. And lonely, too.

Book needed some sprucing up.
Some sunlight.

Some laughter in the rain.

Book needed to
stretch his legs.

Book had a
magnificent time.
So did Emma.

In fact, Book wasn't sure he wanted to go home.

But Emma made sure Book got there, safe and sound.

So maybe Book had a few crumbs in his pages.

A splash or two in his ink.

A smudge at the end.

But Book was surprised to find he didn't mind.

In fact, Book was a little bit proud of his new creases.

It meant Book had been brave.

And returned to tell the tale.

Though, of course, Book still loved his nook.

But at least now Book was excited to make a new friend.

Or two.